WHO TOLD YOU THAT?

Uzi the Bear Goes to School

Written by
Tammy Sanders-Hart

Illustrated by
Kayla Stone

This book is dedicated to my sons, Gerald, Darrian, LJ and Jamal. May you all forever understand that the greater one is within. I love you guys!

Tomorrow is your big day, Uzi." "Your first day of school!", says Dad.
"I know dad but...!", Uzi wants a bumble bee that nearly lands on his nose.
"But, what Uzi?"
"But I've NEVER been to a school before."

Uzi is in deep thought as he and Dad stroll along.
"There will be grizzly bears, lions, and tigers.
I'm just a cub, you know!
My teacher will be mean. No one will be my friend.
I'm afraid to go all by myself, Dad."

"I just imagine and remember when Rory, the beaver, went to school. He didn't like it at all," says Uzi. Uzi plucks a flower and gently sniffs it as he and Dad walk along the trail.

As they continue walking, Uzi imagines all the horrible things that might happen at school.

"We're home," says Dad.
Uzi's mom is cooking dinner in the kitchen.

"Hello, my dears," says Mom. "How was your day?"
"Well ..." Dad begins to speak, but Uzi interrupts him,
"Mom, I don't want to go to school tomorrow."

"Why not?" asks Mom.
"I want to stay home and play in the forest.
I can learn how to hunt for food, defend the family
from predators, gather and store food for the winter,
but Dad does not understand," says Uzi.

"Mom, the forest will make me a strong bear," Uzi growls.
"Yes, dear, the forest will make you a strong bear.
But first, you will go to school to learn how to survive in
the forest. Then you will be a wise bear as well," says Mom.

"Dinner is ready. Go wash your paws and come eat,"
says Mom.

After dinner, Uzi has a bath and then snuggles into bed.
Mom and Dad tuck him in.
"Your first day of school will not be as bad as you imagine,"
said Dad. "I promise!"

"Good night, Uzi."
They watch over Uzi as he drifts off to sleep.
Then they walk out of the room and turn off the light.

While Uzi is sleeping, he has a terrible nightmare
about his first day of school.

Uzi awakes the next morning.
"Rise and shine!" says Dad. "Your big day is here."

Uzi is still afraid of all the bad things that might happen today, but he gets dressed for his first day of school.

"You know, if you keep telling yourself that today is going to be a terrible day, it will be just as terrible as you imagine,"says Dad, "but if you think of all the wonderful things that can happen, today might not be that bad."

Uzi thinks about all the terrible things he imagines
will happen at school. Then he asks himself,
"What if I make a new friend today?
What if there are cubs just like me?
What if my teacher is kind?
I imagine that today might be a good day." Uzi smiles.

Uzi and Dad finally arrive at the school.
They walk into the classroom. Uzi's teacher greets them.
"Hello! What is your name?" she asks.
"My name is Uzi."
"Welcome to class, Uzi. I am so happy you are here,"
says the teacher.

The teacher shakes Dad's hand.
"He's safe with me. See you at 2 pm," the teacher says.

After changing his thoughts, Uzi faces the day
with a different attitude, and his day turns out great.
It is nothing like he imagined.
There are many animals his size. He makes new friends,
and his teacher makes learning fun.

THE END

Made in United States
Orlando, FL
05 July 2022